For Lois

Copyright © 1998 by Scoular Anderson
All rights reserved.
First U.S. edition 1998
Library of Congress Cataloging-in-Publication Data is available.
Library of Congress Catalog Card Number 97-37127
ISBN 0-7636-0443-7
2 4 6 8 10 9 7 5 3 1
Printed in Belgium
This book was typeset in Lucida.
The pictures were done in watercolor and ink.
Candlewick Press
2067 Massachusetts Avenue
Cambridge, Massachusetts 02140

MACPELICAN'S
AMERICAN
ADVENTURE

Scoular Anderson

CANDLEWICK PRESS
CAMBRIDGE, MASSACHUSETTS

Clan MacPelican
Scottish branch

Hector MacPelican
Inventor of extraordinary machines
and head of Clan MacPelican

Esmerelda
Hector's niece

Thomas
Hector's nephew

Aunt Forgetlia
The most forgetful
aunt in the world

Mr. Snoddy the Butler
Likes to keep
things shipshape

Miss Gadget the Mechanic
In charge of finding
the way

Spinner and
Webley, spiders
Stowaways in Aunt
Forgetlia's handbag.
Hope to visit cousins
in Louisiana

Great Uncle Figment
Always seeing strange things.
No one ever believes him
Turpentyne His helper

Mrs. Edibles the Cook
Hasn't smiled for
sixty-four years

It's 1898. Meet the MacPelican clan. They are traveling to the Grand Louisiana Exhibition in the U.S., where Hector MacPelican is to exhibit ten of his newest and finest machines. Hector is so proud of these inventions that he may just have to show them off before they get there. But he should take care . . . Great Uncle Figment is *certain* there's a thief about!

Hector has also invented a special machine for the trip. It's the Dither-Not direction finder, and it will tell them how to get to Louisiana. But what if it doesn't? . . .

The MacPelicans have never been so far away from home before, and they are in for a very puzzling time indeed! Why don't you give them a hand? In every picture you must:

Help Miss Gadget use the Dither-Not direction finder.

Find out if Great Uncle Figment is telling the truth.

Discover what Wilburtina's photographs are of.

Help Thomas and Esmerelda keep an eye on a stranger.

Make sure Spinner and Webley don't get lost on the way.

Help Roxanne round up the ten raccoons.

There are lots of other things to look for too!

Happy journey!

American branch

Wilburtina, Hector's cousin
Her photos never seem quite right

Roxanne
Wilburtina's assistant and raccoon sitter

Wamsutter, Wetumka, and Sweetgrass

Philadelphia and Philharmonia

Muskogee

Pasadena

Deadwood

Musselshell

Skagway

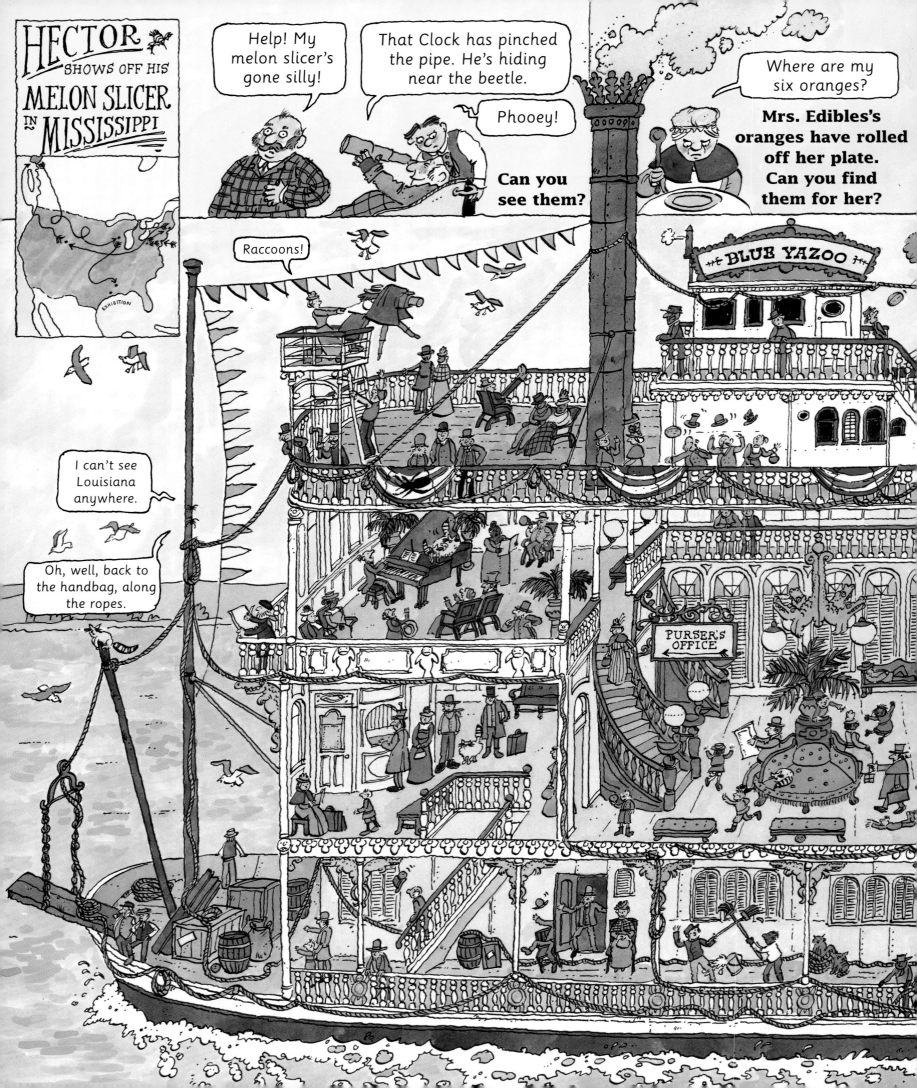